THE EGG POLISHER AND OTHER TALES

T0209648

Funwi F. Ayuninjam

Langaa Research & Publishing CIG
Mankon, Bamenda

Publisher:

Langaa RPCIG
Langaa Research & Publishing Common Initiative Group
P.O. Box 902 Mankon
Bamenda
North West Region
Cameroon
Langaagrp@gmail.com
www.langaa-rpcig.net

Distributed outside N. America by African Books Collective
orders@africanbookscollective.com
www.africanbookcollective.com

Distributed in N. America by Michigan State University Press
msupress@msu.edu
www.msupress.msu.edu

ISBN: 9956-578-20-7

DISCLAIMER
All views expressed in this publication are those of the author and do
not necessarily reflect the views of Langaa RPCIG.

DEDICATION

To the living memory of
My beloved mother
Menge Anna Anwanwen Ayuninjam

Table of Content

ACKNOWLEDGMENTS

I wish here to express my deepest gratitude to all those who made this collection possible. First off I thank my mother, from whom I learned much of what I know of my own first language. She narrated two of the tales. I am very thankful to Mami Julie Tantoh for narrating twelve of them; to Jerry Rawlings Nshuhnkum for narrating four; and to Joseph Che'for Ashing for recounting two. I chanced upon a gentleman, who readily narrated "A Wife's Man"; however, through my imprudence, I did not record his name. I am sorry for this oversight and hope for an opportunity to recognize his contribution publicly.

In transcribing the tales in English, I sought the assistance of several persons in order to ensure as close a correspondence to the original terms and concepts as possible. Here I thank my sister, Mary Nji, my brother, Anthony Ayuninjam as well as my friends Gregory Achu Ashi, Thomas Asongwe, and Francis Tangu Yunishie. Comments from my wife Gwendoline, and my daughter Diane helped me improve various versions of the manuscript—both substantively and editorially. I also owe my gratitude to Bhadraji Jayatilaka, who stepped in late in the process and illustrated the stories. He read each story very keenly before determining how best to depict it in a single pen-and-ink shot. Without the pictures, this book would look very different, very bland.

If I have left out any other contributors to this volume, it was not intentional, and for that I apologize. Ultimately, this book should be the collective pride of the people of Cameroon's North-West Region, whose cultures and mind sets the tales purport to reflect. To them I say thank you.

INTRODUCTION

This collection, albeit the narratives of only a handful of persons, represents folk tradition in the North-West Province of Cameroon. The representation is in terms both of substance and style. Contained herein is a sampling of various human emotions, parental concerns, and societal conflicts: emotional insecurity (A Wife's Man), deceit (The Egg Polisher), obstinacy (The Farmer and the Cannibal), power and control (The Tortoise and the Chief), trickery (Abanda, the Village Menace I & II), malevolence (Revenge of the Coaster), greed (The Tadpole Fisher), jealousy (Dibong, the Jealous Friend), and more. The stylistic representation is reflected in the double writing, as shown by the dialogues, the songs, and the use of choruses.

These tales are ageless, placeless, and, therefore, anonymous; yet they are also the collective wisdom of a people who are supposed once to have walked the planet and communed with other animals and non-animals on the same terms. That is how humans, animals, vegetation, water, and hills/mountains are equally animate and have linguistic expression for their thoughts and sentiments.

Folktales served primarily as entertainment, especially to while the time when families gathered for extensive periods of time for nonintensive activities such shucking groundnuts, corn, and beans in readiness for planting, or shucking pumpkin seeds to grind for a meal. Some of the tales also served as a convenient way of teaching history and culture, and they invariably promoted good listening and speaking skills in the vernacular language as children learned to model the rhetorical patterns of their adult folklorists—with children taking turns night after night till they had gone full circle and then started recounting the same tales over. While the morale of some of the tales is obvious, that of other tales is not; and that, again, is typical both of the traditional mind set and of the educational backdrop of storytelling.

Funwi Ayuninjam
June 2010

THE CRICKET ROASTER
[Narrated by Mami Anna Anwanwen Ayuninjam]

ONCE upon a time, a woman went to harvest peanuts

with her children. While harvesting the peanuts, she dug up crickets and gave them to one of her children to go and roast. Jing--for that was the child's name--went and roasted the crickets in a hut inhabited by an old man. The man asked Jing to cut off the heads for him to taste them. Jing obeyed. He then asked the little boy to give him the tails. Jing again consented and kept chipping off the crickets and serving the old man till they were finished. Pointing to a huge basket, he asked the child to get inside the container and help himself to some fresh meat which would serve him and his mother. Again Jing obeyed and went to the basket, peeped inside, but saw nothing but deep darkness. He put his head into the basket and tried to reach for or feel something, but to no avail. He had just lost his crickets and only source of protein to the old man and would love to return with something in exchange.

Convinced the old man was being very considerate of him and his mother, Jing tried to reach as far into the basket as he could by swinging his hand towards the bottom of the giant container. His head was totally immersed in it, but his legs swung loosely in the air, and his lower abdomen scrubbed hard against the rough edge of the woven basket. After swinging his hand like a pendulum, he still came up empty. The old man told Jing he needed to get into the basket if he wanted anything from it. Jing entered the basket. It was so deep that it fully enclosed him. The old man immediately sealed the basket shut. The boy wailed for help, but his shouts were audible only to his captor, who instantly transformed the basket into a drum for public display and amusement.

Standing on the roadside, the old man targeted farmers returning home after a long day of hard work. As each farmer neared, he offered to play the queen's song in exchange for a triple-crested peanut--the pride of a peanut farmer. Upon receiving it, he had his child captive sing, recounting his plight thus:

Mother sent me to roast crickets,
But I was turned into a musical instrument.
On a mission to roast crickets,
But now I've become a musical instrument.

Farmers listened to the music and continued their homeward journey. Some so enjoyed the melodious voice that they offered two triple-crested peanuts in order to hear the enchanting voice over again. That was the case when Jing's mother came along. When she first heard the music, her heart leapt; she was suspicious, anxious, but unsure. Then she paid to listen once more. After the second performance, she was pretty certain the voice was her son's. She had mixed feelings; she could not betray her identity to the captor, lest he change locations, stop the public displays altogether, or harm her son. She offered to come back on a day of rest so she could more fully enjoy the beautiful music. She then quickly said goodbye to the man and left anxiously.

On the village's traditional day of rest, Jing's mother prepared two dishes: ground *egusi*[*] pudding for her son and a cornmeal paste laced with ground, stinging hot pepper for the old man. She also brought with her two calabashes, one full of honey bees and another empty and perforated. When she arrived the man had the boy sing for her as he had before:

Mother sent me to roast crickets,

---

[*] *egusi: pumpkin seeds*

3

But I was turned into a musical instrument.
On a mission to roast crickets,
But now I've become a musical instrument.

Satisfied it was still her son's voice, she then gracefully served him the cornmeal and hot pepper dish. The gullible and unwary man gratefully accepted the *food* and immediately began to gobble it down hungrily. He never paused one moment to think about what he was eating. Then the pepper began to sting. The avid eater could feel it all over his body--in his fangs, throat, nostrils, eyes, ears, and especially in his sore gums and on his chapped lips. The bemused woman watched with concealed delight. The old man asked her for water.

"Oh water?" she gasped. "Here! Go fetch some water with this calabash." She handed him the perforated pumpkin calabash. He ran to a nearby stream. It was a hot tropical afternoon, and he sweated profusely as he raced off. He got to the stream and found the water clear and sparkling; he was evidently glad he would have his fill. He dipped his calabash into the water. It filled up instantly. He turned around to head back home, concerned about his musical instrument, but no sooner did he take a few steps than the calabash was empty. He raced straight back home and complained to the woman that he could not draw water with her calabash. Ostensibly perplexed, she asked him to go and draw the water from the Royal Wives' Stream. He went there, but still could not come back with water. Again he raced back, and the cunning woman suggested he try the Counselors' Stream. He still could not get a calabashful of water with which to quench his thirst. When he came back this time, the woman asked him to try the King's Stream.

The King's Stream was much further away and while he was gone, the woman fiercely fed her son the *egusi* pudding and took him away. On their way home, she sullied the water from upstream. When the old man saw the brown water he gave up his quest and began running back home to secure his instrument. When he arrived, he opened the door violently and dashed in. The bees let loose by the fleeing mother and child attacked him and stung him to death.

2

ABANDA, THE VILLAGE MENACE I
(OR HOW THE BUSH FOWL CAME TO
HAVE RED MARKS)
[Narrated by Mami Julie Tantoh]

A LONG time ago, Mankah went out in search of a babysitter. She ran into Abanda, who offered to help. Mankah accepted the offer, not knowing that Abanda was a notorious carnivore; indeed he depended solely on other animals for food.

Each week Abanda decapitated and devoured one of Mankah's children. When she came back home to this news, Abanda told her the child was a victim of a day-time cross-border raid. Each week, a child vanished, and with each disappearance came the same explanation. Thus, little by little, Mankah lost all her children.

With all the children gone, Abanda took off in search of another source of nutrition. Mankah, incredulous, went after him. Abanda was more quick footed and stayed ahead of his pursuer, who sang:

Child's best friend,
You have a hand to lend
Stop and take your piece of yam.
Here for you is a piece of yam.

Abanda responded, saying, "I already know you and won't be fooled." He kept running till he was out of Mankah's reach. He then entered a plantation and climbed up one of the palm trees, which he made his home. A few days later, the owner of the plantation came by and found Abanda securely nestled in his palm tree. The farmer asked the intruder,

"Have you been responsible for siphoning my palm-wine all this while?" Before Abanda could utter a word, the farmer began to send a barrage of spears, stones, and sticks towards the thief. Dodging each one of the weapons, Abanda ridiculed the farmer, pointing out that many farmers had tried to capture him like that, but to no avail. He suggested the farmer rather plant the spears into the ground, with the spikes pointing up, so that when the farmer climbed up the tree and shook him loose, he would fall back onto at least one of the spears and, thus, be trapped.

The farmer bought the idea without much consideration. He, thus, surrounded the tree with an inescapable network of spikes, each topped with very hot pepper. He then began climbing up the tree. Abanda had been preparing a large pot of pap for breakfast. As the farmer stretched his hand to reach for the first palm front, Abanda raised the pot and emptied the boiling paste onto the farmer's face. He fell back with a thud and was instantly pinned down by four of his spears. He squealed and groaned in excruciating pain as Abanda climbed down gradually, gave the farmer a mocking wink, and fled.

When Abanda arrived at a clearing, a wild bush fowl saw him and was petrified at the very sight of the much-disliked menace, notorious for his misdeeds and mercilessness. Fearful that he might be an easy meal for Abanda and also aware that Abanda was quick footed, the bush fowl twisted and folded its head under one of its wings and played dead.

Abanda approached the bird, picked him up, and said to himself, "I have eaten all sorts of creatures, but I will *not* eat a dead bush fowl!" That said, he put him back down and proceeded. When Abanda was at a distance, the bush fowl crowed, drawing Abanda's attention. He turned around and came back for the bird, who once more feigned death as he had earlier. Abanda picked him up again and muttered to himself,

"What type of headless creature is this? How can I eat him without the head?"

He left the bird and turned to go when he crowed again, only this time quite mockingly. Abanda said with a broad smile,

"Now I have seen you, and I know exactly how you

look!" When he returned and picked up the bird, he asked, "When I picked you up the first time, where was your head?"

"When I go out, I usually remove my head and keep it at home," said the bush fowl.

"How will you decapitate yourself now?" Abanda sounded more curious than friendly.

The bush fowl gave him a machete with these instructions: "As I dance up in that direction and dance back towards you, sever my head. When I repeat the pattern, reattach my head."

Abanda carried out the bush fowl's instructions accordingly and, rather impressed with the magical results, he implored the bird to teach him the head-off, head-on trick by cutting off and reattaching his head. The bush fowl was only glad to oblige, but asked Abanda to save the dance for some *later* occasion.

As soon as Abanda handed the bush fowl the razor-sharp machete, he severed the scoundrel's head with surgical precision. He stuck the head onto the tip of his spear and displayed it around the village, reassuring everyone he met that Abanda would be a menace no more.

All animals came out with camwood (a red dye) and rubbed it on the bush fowl's paws, legs, and beak to signify its bravery. That is how the bush fowl came to have red marks.

3

THE SONGBIRD AND THE HUNTER (OR HOW A BIRD AND A DOG ENRICHED A FAMILY)

[Narrated by Jerry Rawlings Nshuhnkum]

THERE once lived a woman called Menge. She was so heavy with twins she could no longer go farming. It was planting season, so she asked her daughter, Ntigintum, to sow the seeds that year. Each day she was given seeds for a different crop.

The first day, she was given corn. When she arrived at the farm, she made a little fire, and then fried and ate the corn. While frying the corn, some of the grains dropped to the ground, and a songbird picked them up. This bird planted them and eagerly looked for more loose grains, which it buried into the beds. When Ntigintum returned home, she reported having planted the corn.

The next day, she was given groundnuts to plant. As with the corn, the little girl put her frying pan to personal use by frying and feasting on the groundnuts, while she was ably *assisted* by a bird, which picked up and planted at random the loose groundnuts it found. The farm also had guava trees, pear trees, and bananas trees. When Ntigintum was done, she availed herself of the ripened fruits from these trees. As before, when she returned home, she reported having done well on the farm.

For three more days, the girl set out for the farm – with pumpkin seeds, beans, and Irish potatoes. Consistently, she availed herself of the produce, while a

11

bird helped to plant the seeds. A few weeks later, Menge went into labor and asked Ntigintum to go and find out how the crops were doing. She went out, played with her friends, and returned home with good news about the crops, even though she did not go to the farm.

When weeding season arrived, Ntigintum was asked to go and weed the farm. She went to the farm and was taken aback by the abundance of crops, but she never revealed that she had no hand in the yield. The twins arrived just before harvest season, and Ntigintum was again sent to harvest some raw produce. Menge's farm stood out in the freshness and abundance of its yield compared to her neighbors' farms. Ntigintum filled her basket with a variety of produce: corn, groundnuts, pumpkins, beans, and Irish potatoes. She placed the basket on her head and, as she turned to go, the songbird that had sown the seeds alighted on a tree in the farm and sang:

What your mother gave you to plant
You fried and ate it to your fill.
What your mother gave you to plant
You fried and ate it to your fill.
Maize destined for home, step down and return to the source.
Groundnuts destined for home, step down and return to the
source.
Pumpkins destined for home, step down and return to the
source.
Beans destined for home, step down and return to the source.
Irish potatoes destined for home, step down and return to the
source.

As the bird finished singing, each produce descended from the basket, trailed back to its bed of origin, reattached itself to its stem, and resumed its pre-harvest freshness. The girl, frightened, ran back home and reported her droll experience to her parents. Nobody would believe the account. Incredulous, her father, Tata Ntigintum, threatened her:

"That is a foolish tale. Go to the farm now and bring some food for your mother to cook; and don't you make up another story!"

This time, more frightened of her father than of the experience with the bird, Ntigintum returned to the farm with her basket. As before, she harvested an assortment of fresh produce to fill her basket. The moment she placed it on her head, the bird sang again, and all the produce left her basket.

Ntigintum returned home weeping, certain no one would believe her and fearful her mischief would unravel. When she shared her experience with the rest of the family, her father, as much in disbelief as anger, took his hunting gear – a gun, a spear, and a machete – and followed his daughter to the farm, warning her,

"You dare not be lying to us." Ntigintum was now even more terrified than ever before. When they arrived at the farm, he took his position under a tree overlooking the farm and asked his daughter to go ahead with the harvesting while he observed. She quickly filled her basket and got up to leave when the bird sang again:

What your mother gave you to plant
You fried and ate it to your fill.
What your mother gave you to plant
You fried and ate it to your fill.

Maize destined for home, step down and return to the source.

Groundnuts destined for home, step down and return to the source.

Pumpkins destined for home, step down and return to the source.

Beans destined for home, step down and return to the source.

Irish potatoes destined for home, step down and return to the source.

Dumfounded, Tata Ntigintum walked up close to the bird and said, "What a melodious voice you have! I so love your singing I would like to hear the song once more. I heard it from far away and would love to hear it at close range. May I indulge you?"

The bird readily obliged, came down several branches, and perched on a branch just above the armed man. When the girl filled her basket and tried to leave, the bird sang again; and just as before, the produce gradually made its way from the basket back onto the beds.

Tata Ntigintum told the bird he was quite impressed and invited him to perch on his shoulder, so he might hear even better. The bird alighted on the man's shoulder. Without variation, the girl harvested some farm produce, but could not take a step with it as the bird's melodious tune was followed by the produce returning to the farm. Instantly, the man grabbed the bird and put it in his raffia bag and took it home.

The captive bird now no longer an obstacle to the harvest, Ntigintum harvested and brought back home all the produce: corn, groundnuts, pumpkins, beans, and Irish potatoes. The bird became the provider of first resort. When the family needed cooking oil, Tata Ntigintum turned to the bird, which spat it out. When the family needed salt, the bird provided it similarly. The family turned to the bird even for kitchen utensils – cutlery, pots, and pans. All this while, the bird was in captivity. The man's children were at once fascinated and puzzled by the bird's magical powers.

One day, while the parents were out, the children were in the middle of cooking when they ran out of salt and turned to the bird. Lacking their father's tact, they opened the bag imprudently, and the bird flew off and to freedom. When Tata Ntigintum returned and learned of the children's carelessness, he got them well thrashed and sent them all to retrieve the songbird. They went all over the quarter searching desperately for it. For three days and nights, they combed the farms and bushes, but for three days they came up empty. On the fourth day they ran into a bird catcher and enlisted his help in tracking down their father's bird. They hyperbolized their plight, claiming they risked death if they did not find the bird.

"What type of bird is this," inquired the bird catcher, rather taken by the children's anguish as they looked at one another with consternation. They had not taken a good look at the bird and were uncertain what bird species it was, but one of the children said she thought their father had mentioned a sunbird. The bird catcher, out of sheer pity for the children, caught and handed them a sunbird, which they returned home and placed in their father's bag.

Upon his return, Tata Ntigintum was elated to learn that his bird was back. He hurriedly removed it from the bag and demanded cooking oil; none was forthcoming. He asked for salt; the bird was equally reticent. Taking the improvidence for defiance, the man shut the door and window and, using a stick, hit the bird on the head, legs, and wings repeatedly. The bird pleaded for mercy—offering to entertain the family with melodious tunes, but to no avail. Tata Ntigintum was so vexed and sadistic he gave the bird a blow to the throat saying, "You were *not* brought here to sing! Will your music fill our stomachs?"

Exhausted and disabled, the sunbird asked his captor breathily, "Finish me off by roasting me for dinner. You would also put me out of my misery."

Tata Ntigintum eagerly complied and roasted the bird. As soon as he did, the bird said,

"Eat me, and make sure that no one else partakes of the meal."

Again, Tata Ntigintum heeded the bird's instructions and devoured him greedily. When he was finished, the bird said from the man's stomach,

"Go to an open clearing and defecate me. Do not use a pit latrine."

Tata Ntigintum went to the backyard and, as he began to defecate, a puppy emerged. The dog grew to be just as gluttonous as it was beautiful. It had an insatiable appetite for food, but it was severely stunted and looked only like a puppy. This dog was, however, the best hunting dog in the village, and had no rival. Whenever Tata Ntigintum and the dog went out hunting, the man took the dog's counsel on hunting and increasingly depended on the counsel.

One day, as they readied to head out for a hunting expedition, the dog told his master, "Today I will take my guitar with me and will play it while sitting in a tree. My music will lure game of various types. Do *not* shoot the lions, elephants, or deer. You may hunt down the rat-moles, the porcupines, and the hares." When they arrived at the forest, as agreed, the dog began to play his guitar to these lyrics:

Animals of the wild, come on out!
Animals of the wild, come on out!
Animals of the wild, come on out!

Upon hearing the song, a column of animals began to stream out of a trail and head towards the tree meekly. First came the lions, followed by the elephants, the zebras, and the deer. Tata Ntigintum was tempted as he lay in hiding behind a thicket at a slight elevation, his rifle pointing at the animals. When rat-moles, porcupines, and hares emerged, he took aim at a giant rat-mole and fired pam! As the rat-mole dropped dead, so did all the preceding animals.

Tata Ntigintum rushed back home and enlisted the help of his neighbors, with whom he slaughtered the animals. He then threw a big feast for the entire village. Everyone who came had his or her fill, but many wondered about Tata Ntigintum's magnanimity. Some asked,

"*How* did he catch so many animals in a single day when other hunters could barely catch a single animal?"

One day, his brother, Ndam Tata, came to him for help:

"I am planning a big celebration and need a lot of meat. May I use your hunting dog?"

"I am afraid you might not feed it appropriately. My dog is a glutton, and when he starves, he does not cooperate," the man said.

His brother persisted, vowing to do right by the dog and threatening his brother with responsibility should his event fail.

"I cannot let your event fail! You understand what it

takes to work with this dog. Here!" Tata Ntigintum handed his brother the dog and wished him luck.

The sun was already hot over the village, even though it was only mid-morning. Quick-footed Ndam Tata was, nonetheless, anxious to cover much ground as he and the dog still had to cross Ntah Ngu, a treacherous mountain range, before getting to Alileng, the hunting ground.

Before noon the dog was tired and could no longer keep pace with Ndam Tata, who had not slowed down since they departed. The dog had not eaten all morning. Even when they got to a brook, and the dog tried to lap a little water to quench his thirst, the eager hunter pulled on the leash impatiently, and the dog yielded.

The sun was well overhead when the hunter and the dog arrived in Alileng. It was cooler, and only a few steaks of sunrays pierced through the giant, aging trees and their innumerable descendants. Ndam Tata was hungry, but had brought only his cola-nuts, which he began to masticate. The dog was famished, but had no choice. He gave the hunter these instructions:

"I will climb up that tree and begin to sing a song, accompanied by my guitar. Many animals will come out. Do not shoot the large ones; rather, target the small ones, like the rat-moles, the porcupines, and the hares."

"Alright!" said the hunter, as he took cover behind a giant root that rose so high it could conceal him entirely. For disguise, he broke a large tree branch and covered himself with its broad fresh leaves. Then the dog began to sing:

Animals of the wild, come on out!
Animals of the wild, come on out!
Animals of the wild, come on out!

Once more, and with docility, the animals began to head out of a trail, led by lions and followed by elephants. Seeing the elephants, Ndam Tata said to himself angrily,

"I am here to hunt for a big event. Why should I leave an elephant and shoot a rat-mole? How many persons can a rat-mole feed?" Ignoring the dog's instructions, the young hunter gunned down one of the elephants with a single blast to the skull. The rest of the animals raced up the tree, brought down the dog, and pulled him by his extremities all the way to a nearby pond, where they dropped him. Because he was famished and had fractures on all legs, he could not swim to safety.

Ndam Tata raced back home and reported the dog had fallen into a pond. Tata Ntigintum was enraged and would not accept his brother's explanations and pleading.

"You must bring back my dog," he insisted. "No other dog in the village, no matter how beautiful, can replace that one. I want only my dog!"

Puzzled, Ndam Tata assembled a large number of men of varying heights to help him rescue the dog. For each man he prepared recompense commensurate with his height. The tallest helpers, whom he expected to contribute the most towards the rescue, would each receive a ram, a gourd of palm-wine, and baskets of *achu*. The short men would together receive a goat, some snacks, and a few gourds of palm-wine.

When the tall men arrived at the pond, they huddled to strategize, and then sang laughingly:

Little doggie without limbs,
Is mud more comforting than home?
Little wise dog that was beguiled,
Come out and seek our guidance.
Little brave hunter without a heart,
There is no lion here to scare you!

Their leader threw into the pond a long bamboo. Another man jumped into the standing water and searched in vain for the dog.

Disappointed, they huddled again, sang, and danced at the edge of the pond, and threw in the bamboo. A second tall rescuer jumped in, but came up empty. The men repeated the pattern three more times, but three times again their efforts yielded no positive results. The men were exhausted and, as night was fast approaching, called off the search and asked everyone to return home.

"I will try," said a short man. Most of the onlookers were surprised at the offer.

"What can *you* do that we have been unable to do?" asked one of the tall men quizzically.

Without pleading their case, the short men all gathered around the pond while everyone else looked on with indignation. One of the men led a high-pitched chant directed at the dog:

Lead:	*Beloved son of the soil!*
Chorus:	*What is your grief?*
	Come out and tell us your grief!

Lead:	*Protector and pride of the land!*
Chorus:	*What is your grief?*
	Come out and tell us your grief!

Lead:	*Beloved hunter of the village!*
Chorus:	*What is your grief?*
	Come out and tell us your grief!

Lead:	*Guitar player without a parallel!*
Chorus:	*What is your grief?*
	Come out and tell us your grief!

By the time the singing was over, the lead singer was in tears as he was taken by his earnestness. While still in tears, he threw the bamboo into the pond and held on to one end. Everyone gathered around the pond and watched eagerly. Within moments, the dog appeared, clinging tightly to the bamboo. The rescuer pulled the dog to safety and, turning to Ndam Tata, said,

"Didn't you set aside more food and drinks for the tall men than for us because you underestimated us?" That said, he turned around and dropped the dog back into the pond and led his friends away.

To appease the disgruntled men, Ndam Tata slaughtered a buffalo for them. They were served a delectable dinner of *fufu* and yams with *ndole* and *egusi* sauces. There was plenty of palm-wine—each man drinking from his own calabash gourd. The banquet lasted well into the night, and as the men readied to leave, they were each given a gourdful of palm-wine and a basket of food to take home to their families.

News of the short men's feat spread quickly throughout the village, and when the short men returned to the pond the next morning, a huge crowd had gathered to witness the performance. As before, they sang imploringly:

| Lead: | *Savior of Tata Ntigintum's family!* |

| Chorus: | *What is your grief?* |
| | *Come out and tell us your grief!* |

Lead:	*Model counselor of the hunter!*
Chorus:	*What is your grief?*
	Come out and tell us your grief!

Lead:	*God's gift to the land!*
Chorus:	*What is your grief?*
	Come out and tell us your grief!

Lead:	*The counselor who never errs!*
Chorus:	*What is your grief?*
	Come out and tell us your grief!

As before, one of the men threw in a bamboo and, as before too, out of the water came the dog, clinging to the bamboo tightly. The men handed the dog to Ndam Tata, who would not stop thanking them. Tata Ntigintum, for his part, was most glad to be reunited with his dog and vowed never more to lend him to anyone.

4

THE TADPOLE FISHER
(OR THE WOMAN WHO PREFERRED
TADPOLES TO HER DAUGHTER)
[Narrated by Jerry-Rawlings Nshuhnkum]

ONCE upon a time a woman named Lum went fishing for tadpoles with her daughter Bih. They left before dawn, so the waters would be calm and clear. After toiling for several hours, they caught no tadpoles; only little crabs had entered their calabash traps. They persisted, but their efforts yielded the same unsatisfactory results.

"What might be the matter?" the woman asked herself in wonderment. "I have caught tadpoles here many times before," she said to the child reassuringly. Bih had no doubt. Hoping for different results, the couple persisted.

It was mid-afternoon, and some of the farmers who had seen the mother-daughter pair earlier were already returning home. The look of bewilderment on the women's faces said it all: This woman must be crazy! But they dare not say it. They, however, burst out laughing like children once they were out of earshot of the couple.

It was sunset, but Lum had not given up her search for tadpoles. As she pushed aside a large piece of rock at the edge of the stream, Mamiwater stuck her head out and asked, "Do you know why you've been unable to catch tadpoles?"

"No. Please tell me. I really want to know,' Lum replied.

"If you really want to know, push your daughter into that pool," she said, pointing to a huge, dark pool of water.

During the dry season, the pool was a favorite playground for children, especially those who were still learning to swim. In the rainy season, the water was treacherous, and children were forbidden from swimming there. It had been raining heavily for months, and the pool was so full the runoff into the stream had a strong current.

"My daughter does not swim well, and I fear she might drown," pleaded Lum.

"You must choose between your fears and knowledge of how to catch tadpoles," Mamiwater responded with a sadistic grin. "I guarantee that you will have an abundant harvest, but only if you let your daughter go. If you don't want to, stop wasting your time and go home."

Lum was in a quandary. Bih was her only daughter; yet she had a big dinner for which she needed to prepare a tadpole dish. She was reputed in the village for that dish, which would be served to the elders. Preferring not to fail her guests, she moved up close to Bih and opened her arms. The little girl was exhausted and welcomed her mother's embrace. Lum instantly flung her into the pool. The child screamed in fright as she plunged headlong and helplessly into the water and vanished instantly.

When Lum returned to her traps, they were each full of tadpoles, which she eagerly poured into porous woven baskets. The catch was so plentiful she disposed of some of the tadpoles. As darkness fell, she headed home.

Upon arriving home, news of her masterful harvest had spread like wildfire, although her husband's immediate concern was for their daughter. Lum said she had asked her to return home before darkness in order to start preparing dinner. Azewo, her husband, stared at her with fury and said in a quaking voice,

"We have not seen her!" Lum looked at him shiftily, and then he boomed, "*Where* is Bih?" Lum still would not respond as she cupped a hand in another as if she wanted to request a favor.

"Have you lost your voice?" he asked, looking at his wife. "No one will sleep in this house till we have found Bih," Azewo threatened.

They all went out in search of the girl, knocking on people's doors in the quarter as they headed towards the stream. The sky was clear, the air still, and the entire village sound asleep safe for the Azewo household as they searched for Bih in the fields that sandwiched the narrow path to the stream. At midnight they all returned home.

At the crack of dawn, they resumed their futile search. Azewo had notified the village chief of the missing child, so a team of men from the royal palace joined the family and many other neighbors and volunteers in the search. After one week of tireless, yet fruitless, work, the chief officially called off the search and declared the child dead and the loss an abomination.

A farewell ceremony was organized for Bih at which seven royal counselors performed an appeasement ritual. The seven men represented the girl's age. Because she was premature, the chief could not attend the event. In order to forestall a recurrence of this abomination, the chief retired the child's name by decreeing that no newborn child could be named *Bih* in the entire village.

There were lots of tadpoles for use at Bih's funeral celebration, and those that could not be used were placed on mats to dry outside when the sun came out. They were taken back into the kitchen when the sun began to go down.

One day a charcoal burner, a neighbor of Azewo, went about searching for wood and wound up at the stream where Bih vanished. As he was splitting his wood, the child came up close to the surface of the water and sang:

Go-getter of renown...oh ching
Upon your return home, tell my father...oh ching
That my mother is a wicked woman...oh ching
She pushed me into a pool of water...oh ching
I am a babysitter for a witch...oh ching
I am her achu pounder...oh ching
I am her fufu pounder...oh ching
I am her clothe washer...oh ching
My mother is a wicked woman...oh ching

The charcoal burner moved closer to the sound source and asked her to sing for him again, claiming he had not heard her clearly. Once more she sang, and her voice was quite distinctly Bih's. Perplexed, he abandoned his work and headed straight to Azewo's home, where Azewo was weaving a giant raffia bag. Whizzing and barely able to contain himself, he told Azewo about the worrisome song, adding, "I could not see anybody, but please come with me in case you can make sense of the song."

Azewo sighed and replied, "I am in the middle of this project, and I cannot stop now."

"I can see that you are busy," his neighbor conceded, "but this is very important and urgent. Why don't you come and see it for yourself?"

Azewo abandoned his work reluctantly and followed his neighbor. When they got to the stream, the charcoal burner asked Azewo to hide by the stream while he worked. Shortly after he began splitting his wood, the voice came up again and sang ruefully:

Go-getter of renown...oh ching
Upon your return home, tell my father...oh ching
That my mother is a wicked woman...oh ching
She pushed me into a pool of water...oh ching
I am a babysitter for a witch...oh ching
I am her achu pounder...oh ching
I am her fufu pounder...oh ching
I am her clothe washer...oh ching
My mother is a wicked woman...oh ching

Go-getter of renown...oh ching
Upon your return home, tell my father...oh ching
...

"That is Bih's voice!" Azewo exclaimed wildly as the girl started singing again. "There's no doubt about it!" Hearing her father's voice, the girl stopped singing and returned into the water. The two men returned home and sought after the best medicine-men in the land who might help them rescue the girl. They identified both tall and short men and promised to reward them accordingly—the tall men earning more that the short men.

The next day the medicine-men returned to the stream. The tall men rubbed various portions on their staff, and one of them threw it into the pool. The child did not appear. The men modified the portions, rubbed them on the staff, and massaged it as if it were a living being. Then their leader raised it above his right shoulder and said, "You are our envoy and represent the tall and strong of the land. Don't let us down." He then threw the staff into the pond diagonally. Everybody waited anxiously, but the child still did not emerge. He turned reluctantly to one of the short men and invited him to come and throw his staff. This was only a perfunctory request as the short people were thought to be of no consequence.

The short man walked up to the end of the pond very confidently, spun his staff over his head prestodigitally, and threw it with minimal force. The staff landed vertically but with almost no splash and disappeared into the water right away. There was grave silence as all onlookers suddenly huddled around the pond and stretched their necks to peer into the water for any results. Moments later, Bih appeared wearing a beautiful dress and a broad, innocent smile. The dress was the same one she wore when she last came there with her mother.

Azewo hoisted her into the air ecstatically and performed a swagger more commonly seen in women, while saying melodiously,

God never sleeps!
No one can stool for another!
Your destiny is yours alone!

The crowd responded in ear-shattering and ceaseless cheering. He immediately gave the short medicine-men everything they requested for their services and led the crowd away.

That evening Mamiwater waited in vain for her babysitter and sent a toad to find out what might have gone wrong. The toad went to Azewo and sang:

My mother has asked
That you give her a bag of cowries.

If not, return the tadpoles.

Outraged, Azewo responded:
"We are at war, but all you have to offer is a big, loud mouth. Get out of here with your pot-belly!"

The toad returned and reported the insulting reception. Mamiwater sent a chameleon on the same mission, and with the same message:

My mother has asked
That you give her a bag of cowries.
If not, return the tadpoles.

Azewo responded, "You sluggish being! Don't make me kick you!"

The chameleon went back and reported Azewo's threatening response. The next envoy was a lizard, whom Azewo mocked:

"Since when did you have teeth? Get out of here!"

When Mamiwater heard of this dismissive behavior, she wondered, "The toad and the chameleon might have been spited due to their sluggishness. Why would he treat you with the same scorn? I will handle this matter myself." She went to see Azewo, but he refused to admit her into his house, saying he would not receive a devil's daughter.

Upset, Mamiwater emptied the stream and the pool, channeling the water to Azewo's compound, which was inundated up to the roof. All medicine-men in the village tried in vain to get rid of the water.

Two weeks later, a soothsayer came and asked Azewo to place all the tadpoles back into the water. As soon as the tadpoles were emptied into the flood water, the water receded into the stream and the pool, restoring the compound to its pre-flood state, except for the hearth, which still had a pool of water the size of a medium pot. Azewo's household was still beleaguered as the man wondered:

"With all the tadpoles disposed of, why is there still water in the hearth? We need Mamiwater back here!" He sent one of his sons to go and appeal for her help. Mamiwater did not receive the boy kindly, telling him,

"Your father treated my envoys callously, drove me from his compound, but now wants me to help him? He must take me for a fool. Go and tell him I am no fool!"

That afternoon, Azewo committed all his children to searching for any remaining tadpoles. They found one lodged in their mother's bag. Azewo gave Lum a murderous look as she handed him the tadpole. As soon as he dropped it into the pond, the water wiggled out with the tadpole and back to its source. Life began to return to normal in the family.

5

ABANDA, THE VILLAGE MENACE II
[Narrated by Mami Julie Tantoh]

ABANDA, a little dog, caught and ate a baby elephant. The elephant's parents were in mourning when a tortoise came by and asked them in consternation:

"Can't you catch Abanda? You can't be this powerless before a dog! I will get him if you want me to," the tortoise offered. The elephants readily agreed. They also agreed to feed the tortoise nothing but *egusi** pudding during the entrapment.

Two days later, the tortoise went to Abanda's and, pointing to the dog's black feces, said the blackness was a sign of poor nutrition. To prove his point, the tortoise defecated in front of his counterpart and asked him to taste the little whitish-yellowish mound. Abanda did and loved it. Indeed he so liked it that he ate it all, and then asked the tortoise,

"What type of food do you eat to produce such tasty feces? I would like to have some more if you can defecate again."

---

* *egusi: pumpkin seeds*

35

The tortoise obliged and produced some more excrement, which Abanda gobbled down with appetite. Abanda longed for more, and the tortoise obliged further, but this time only a few pellets came out, which

Abanda devoured quickly and wanted more. Because the tortoise's anus hurt from the effort, he had Abanda put his finger in the tortoise's anus and scoop up more feces.

As Abanda fed from the tortoise's anus, the tortoise told him he was running late for a function and that Abanda had to follow him. Thus, Abanda followed the tortoise while feeding from his anus. As the two approached the village gathering place, other animals came out and burst out laughing at the spectacle. As the tortoise himself began to laugh, his sphincter weakened, and he let loose Abanda, who scrammed in shame. The tortoise was displeased and warned his co-conspirators:

"I will discontinue the effort to catch Abanda if you facilitate his escape and make me look foolish."

The next day the tortoise lured Abanda into the same trap. As the previous day, Abanda followed the tortoise till they reached the gathering place. The other animals cut off the path, and then surrounded and captured the menace. He had no chance to plead his case and was trampled to death by the elephants.

6

THE EGG POLISHER
(OR HOW A WATER BUFFALO LOST HER
EGGS AND A CHIEF HIS LIFE)
(Narrated by Mami Julie Tantoh)

THERE once lived a man called Mebifor, whose friend was a water buffalo. One day Mebifor went into the bush and returned with the eggs of a chameleon. He polished them till they shone, and then he showed them to the water buffalo, saying he could polish her own eggs as well so they would shine like his.

The water buffalo said she would take Mebifor up on his offer. As requested, the water buffalo brought Mebifor palm oil and salt. Mebifor, with chameleon eggs hidden in his bag, told the water buffalo she could not watch him at close range while he performed his craft of polishing eggs. She had to observe from upstream, way uphill.

In reality, Mebifor was no egg polisher; he was a complete phony. As he began frying the water buffalo's eggs, he feared the water buffalo might come out of the water and uncover his deceit, so he took out one of the chameleon eggs and said out loud,

Wa gebi Mebifor!
Wa gebi Mebifor!

Even without understanding the gibberish, the water buffalo responded,
Hold it just like that, Mebifor!

39

Ever gradually, Mebifor fried all the water buffalo's eggs and put them in his bag. In their place, Mebifor left the chameleon eggs and took off for a distant land. The water buffalo pursued him. As she closed in on him, he uttered a spell repeatedly:

Miss my foot and bite a tree trunk!
Miss my foot and bite a tree trunk!

The hex worked, and the water buffalo sank her teeth into a giant tree stump and remained stuck till Mebifor was out of sight. Then the water buffalo was liberated. She resumed the chase till she was on Mebifor's heels, when Mebifor screamed again,

Miss my foot and bite a tree trunk!
Miss my foot and bite a tree trunk!

As before, the water buffalo suddenly found herself biting a tree stump while the egg polisher escaped into a neighboring village, where there was a big end-of-year cultural performance. The chief was in attendance, and Mebifor secured a seat next to him. A little later, he took out one of the buffalo eggs and ate it, and then turned to the chief and asked him what he ate, mocking his entourage for starving their leader. That said, he took out one of the eggs and handed it the chief, saying, "That is food for chiefs!"

The chief ate it and loved it very much. "Where did you find such an egg," he inquired. Mebifor responded quizzically,

"You hid your scrota and want me to fry mine and share them with you because you are so afraid of death?"

"Do you mean to say this is your scrotum?" The

chief was quite stunned.

"When I travel and become hungry, I remove a scrotum and fry it for dinner. As I came to your annual festival, I thought I should have my scrotum to share with you."

"What do you suggest we do now," asked the chief. Mebifor responded eagerly,

"I would be glad to remove and fry your scrota if you so desire."

"Let's go to my living quarters," the chief offered with excitement. He also asked his staff not to accompany him. It was uncustomary for the chief to go anywhere alone, but he insisted his guards stay back and enjoy the celebration. When the two men arrived in the private residential area, Mebifor instructed the chief:

"Climb to the ceiling, cut open a hole, and sit down, letting your scrota jut out through the hole. I will take care of the rest."

The chief, notorious for arguing, somehow followed Mebifor's orders without giving them a second thought. The egg polisher, using a sharp machete, slashed off the chief's testicles with surgical precision. The chief almost went mad with pain as he jumped around the attic till he slipped and fell to the floor with a heavy thud. The chief was a hefty man, and his fall was so loud people in the adjoining building heard it and came rushing to find out what caused the noise. Mebifor stopped the onslaught at an outer entrance and assured them all was fine and that the chief would soon rejoin them. Leading them back to the dance area, he took one of the drums and led everyone in a new song:

Harvester of a water buffalo's eggs
Has cut the scrota of a foreign chief

41

Who wants to dance, but can't stand on his legs.
We dance and rejoice with a renowned thief.

Harvester of a water buffalo's eggs
Has cut the scrota of a foreign chief
Who wants to dance, but can't stand on his legs.
We dance and rejoice with a renowned thief.

. . .

Everyone danced to this new song till darkness fell. They so enjoyed the new dance they forgot about their chief. When they returned to his private quarters, he was dead. Mebifor had vanished without a trace.

7

A WIFE'S MAN
[Unknown Narrator]

ONCE upon a time there lived a man and a woman who had an only son. When he grew up, they found him a bride, and he got married. He was very hardworking right from his youth, but after he married, be began to cater only to his wife. When he hunted for and brought back game, he gave it all to his wife and ignored his parents. Even as his parents were old and improvident, the son kept providing only for his wife. Having warned him repeatedly about being completely reliant on a woman the man decided to teach his son a lesson about being henpecked.

One day the young bride readied to go farming, and the man asked his son to keep an eye on his wife till she was out of sight. Once she disappeared from his view, the son reported to his father, who asked him,

"Didn't you say you loved your wife so much that you could not attend to any of my needs?"

Looking down in embarrassment, the son confirmed. His father instructed him to go into the goat barn and bring out one of the fresh-looking goats. When his son came out with the goat, the old man asked his son to take the goat to the backyard and slaughter it. When he slaughtered the goat, his father asked him to pour the blood into a hole in the backyard. Following his father's instructions, he skinned the goat, prepared the meat for drying, and dumped the skin into another hole in the backyard.

When the young bride returned from the farm, she saw the blood stains in the backyard and asked her husband how they came about. He gave her his father's concocted version: He had tried in vain to recover a debt from a friend, so killed and buried him there. His father had asked him to hold on to this explanation for a few days and then come back to him.

The following week a dispute erupted between the

44

young couple, which the son took to his father for resolution. The man asked him,

"Are you truly angry today?" The son said yes.

"Didn't you say you loved your wife?" the man pursued. When your wife goes farming, stay at home. When she returns, ask her for bath water. If she hesitates, spank her in order to drive home the message that a man cannot let a woman control him.

As the young lady returned from the farm, the husband asked her for bath water.

"I'll do so, right after I get started on preparing dinner."

The man may not have heard her fully, but immediately pounced on her and gave her a good beating for being disobedient. He easily overpowered her because he was physically strong, whereas she was quite petite and tired from a day's farm work.

When neighbors heard the crying and came to find out why, she was reeling on the front yard and referring to her husband as a murderer. As proof, she pointed to the blood stains and the *grave* in the backyard.

The chief was informed of the *crime* and sent his counselors to investigate the matter right away. However, the dig did not unearth a corpse, so they went away.

The son later visited with his father, who asked him,

"Will you now listen to me, or give all your attention to your wife?"

He fell on the old man's feet, asked for his forgiveness, and assured him that he fully trusted and relied on his father.

8

THE FARMER AND THE APES
[Narrated by Mami Julie Tantoh]

THERE once lived a farmer called Fru, who had a large banana and plantain plantation. To protect the farm from thieves, whenever he finished working, he stayed there and guarded it himself while playing xylophones. Whenever he played, apes came out of a neighboring forest and danced to the melodious tunes. Fru would tap fresh palm-wine and share it with the apes, who were indeed the greatest of the thieves. The farmer ingratiated himself and made the apes so friendly to him they stopped stealing his ripening bananas and plantains.

One day, as they were all having fun drinking and dancing, Fru asked his ape friends,

"As I am playing this music to your delight, if one day you came here and found me dead, what would you do?"

One ape said he would stab himself to death. Two more apes concurred with their friends. One day the man slaughtered a goat and took its blood and entrails to the farm. As before, he played his music, and when he sensed that the apes might be approaching, he lay on the ground facing up, placed a blood-stained knife by his side, robbed the blood all over his body, laid the entrails over his abdomen, and feigned death.

The first ape to arrive on the scene was so taken by sadness he picked up the knife and stabbed himself to death. The second one arrived and exclaimed,

"This is unbelievable! My friend dead?!" He too took his life by stabbing himself. The third and fourth apes followed suite. When the fifth got to the scene, he was shocked at the tragedy, but took a step back to examine the catastrophe, and then wondered to himself,

"Is this how a person lies when he is dead? He appears to be breathing!" The ape retreated gently into the forest and got a solid piece of stick. He returned and moved ever stealthily towards the man, and then gave him a solid lash. The man almost went mad with pain as he jumped up, screamed loudly, and squeezed his buttocks while jumping around like a kangaroo. The ape ran up a tree. When he recovered from the pain, the farmer picked up the four carcasses, hung them on a bamboo, and headed home.

9

DIBONG, THE JEALOUS FRIEND
[Narrated by Joseph Che'for Ashing]

THERE once lived two friends, Bim and Dibong. They came from neighboring homes. Bim came from a wealthy family, while Dibong was from a lowly and needy home. Bim's mother always cooked bounteous meals; everyone at table had more than enough to eat; and Bim looked healthy and happy. Dibong, on the other hand, barely had anything to eat on a regular basis. His mother often depended on her neighbors' leftovers-- over which she and her family feasted. Needless to say, Dibong did not always look healthy or cheerful, although he largely accepted his lot.

With time, however, Dibong grew increasingly jealous of Bim and wished his friends and family could fall into misfortune, so he does not look left out. "How can I kill his mother so there would be no one left to cater so well to him?" he thought.

One day as these friends went playing and bird hunting, Dibong revealed his scheme: "Pal, you know that our friendship is too great to be broken by anyone-- even our parents. But you also know that lately our mothers have foiled our plans for afternoon fun by making either of us run silly errands. Wouldn't it be wonderful if we could do away with them, so we can live and play freely?" Bim's eyes widened as he was totally stupefied at the thought of living without his mother.

"But where shall we find food, and who will cook it for us?"

"There will always be food--maybe not as plentiful as we would like, but we can always make do with whatever we come by. We *are* men, aren't we?" Bim stared into emptiness, still amazed, but somewhat less apprehensive about Dibong's thought that life might not change appreciably without their mothers.

"But how shall we kill our parents?" Bim inquired.

"No problem! I have a good and simple plan."

It was a lovely afternoon. The sun was hot, the sky blue, and the shed trees full of birds' nests. Bim looked up and saw a sunbird perched on nearby tree branch. It held a piece of fresh straw firmly in its beak. It then spun around the branch, as if to ensure privacy, and then alighted on a half-completed nest. Dibong's momentary silence caught the attention of his friend, who then followed him with his eyes to the scene in the tree. Dibong took out his catapult and a rounded pebble, anchored the pebble, and looked up at a kingfisher- now working on its nest with excitement. He aimed and plugged it from its beak. It dropped instantly, even without flapping its wings.

Bim was evidently proud of his friend's dexterity as he came back with his tenth bird of the day. He looked at him with admiration and said, "Dibong, you're so good at this! You've caught twice as many birds as I."

In a humbling tone, Dibong replied, "But I've been hunting for twice as long as you. I assure you that you will get better. Just be patient and listen to me more."

Bim found Dibong more trustworthy and asked him for particulars about the scheme to murder their mothers.

"That is very easy. We shall take our mothers to the river. I shall take mine upstream, and you will take yours downstream. The moment the running water turns red, know that I have killed my mother; then you too should kill yours. Clear?" Bim nodded in agreement. They both walked home feeling ostensibly resolute, although deeply apprehensive. Hardly did either of them utter a word, but as they approached their homes and were about to part company, Dibong turned to Bim and said, "How about tomorrow? Wouldn't noon be a good time? That is when our mothers usually accompany us to the river for a swim." Bim looked tense, but grinned in a half-nod. His head remained down as he turned to go.

Dibong spent most of the following morning on the porch grinding camwood, a reddish chalk commonly used for religious rituals. He reduced it to ash, so it could easily liquefy. He had worked largely without notice as his mother was out in the backyard trimming the withering banana leaves. Dibong had hoped to answer no questions about his quiet, messy job, but as he finished cleaning up, his mother returned. In a panic, he shunted the bucketful of camwood into an opening between bricks that were stacked against the wall on the porch. Dibong's blood red hands, however, caught his mother's eyes.

"Dibong, what is the matter with you? Why are your hands red?" Dibong was at a loss for words and began scratching his head when his mother stormed, "Go and wash them quickly! And don't take that blood up to your hair again." Camwood, by virtue of its color, was sometimes referred to as blood.

Dibong used up all the water he had drawn from the river but still could not rid his hands of the "blood." It was mid-day, and his mother asked him to go to the river and wash his hands properly and draw some water. Dibong was clearly elated and relieved at the thought of going away. At the same time, Bim came by to say he and his mother were on their way to the river. Dibong had two water gourds as he headed to the river; one contained the camwood powder.

As arranged, Bim led his mother downstream. As soon as Dibong arrived at the river, he quickly rinsed his hands, drew water in a gourd, and dropped the other gourd into the river. The calabash initially hit a stone and shattered into pieces, letting loose its deceptive contents. Upon dissolving, the ash instantly turned the fast-flowing sparkling water bright red. Dibong picked up his gourd of water and quickly ran back home.

Bim and his mother were still downstream filling their water gourds when the water suddenly turned blood red. Bim's mother looked at her son in wonderment and exclaimed, "What might be going on upstream?!" They had filled three gourds, so she asked her son to come into the river and help her take ashore the clean water they had fetched. Seeing the colored water, Bim concluded that his friend had kept his promise; it was then his turn to honor his own part of the bargain. As his mother tried to step out of the water, Bim drew an axe he had been hiding and lunged at her. She screamed helplessly as Bim instantly decapitated her and dumped her body in the stream.

As soon as Dibong arrived home, he rushed his mother out of the house and into a shack he had built in a huge shade tree. He did not offer her any explanation for the emergency. He angrily refused his mother's nervous requests that he come clean on the bizarre goings-on. He left her alone and climbed down the tree. Satisfied with his masterful scheme, Dibong said to himself, "No matter how little food my mother gives me, and no matter how tasteless it may be, I will still enjoy it knowing that no one is better off than I. As a matter of fact, Bim will have nothing at all; I just could not stand his excesses in the face of my endless privation. So long, rich pal!"

Bim returned to a cold house. He missed his mother, but relished his friendship with Dibong that he feared his mother might jeopardize. But then he thought to himself, "My mother loved me, and I always had my way with her. Wouldn't she have given me all the time I needed to be with Dibong had I asked her?" This was a good question, but it came too late, far too late. He had never had to take care of himself, and, for the first time, breakfast, lunch, and dinner would be all on him. That thought scared him. For now, though, there were still lots of supplies to keep him going for a fortnight.

In the days that followed, the two friends were out playing as usual, and both seemed excited about their new-found license. But by the end of the first week, Bim increasingly discerned a pattern in his playmate. This pattern became much clearer during his third week as an orphan, when he had run out of all food supplies; yet his companion did not look as hungry as he. Bim noticed that each day around noon, Dibong asked to be alone. When he left, he never returned home but hovered for a while around a huge tree in the distance. Whenever he came back, he didn't look as hungry and haggard as he was when he left.

One day, Bim wondered to himself as he saw Dibong leaving, "What might there be of such interest under that tree as to keep my friend going back there so regularly? And he never fails! Why can't I come?" These were puzzling questions to which he couldn't figure out answers as quickly as he wanted, so he decided to pace his friend the next day.

"My friend, stay right here. I'll be back shortly," he

said as he took off for the shade tree. As usual, Bim consented with a nod, but no sooner was the sly out of sight than Bim took off after him, following the same footpath. As Bim approached the huge tree, he heard his scheming friend singing a song. He always sang this song as a signal to his conspiring mother as a request for lunch. Bim had never heard the song before, and listened quietly and intently as his crafty pal sang:

Mother, Mother, give me food to eat
And then of Bim I will go ask:
"Where have you left your mother?"

Upon hearing this song and recognizing her son's voice, Dibong's mother threw him lunch wrapped in a bundle. He sat under the tree and gulped it down quickly while his gullible friend gnashed his teeth and lamented,

"So my friend has tricked me into beheading my mother while he still enjoys the caring company and the love of his? And she too is going along with this evil plot? Well, I will make sure my *friend* has his due." Bim left, his face drawn, for his heart was full of remorse, anguish, and rage.

One week had passed since gullible Bim eavesdropped on cunning Dibong, and for one week Bim was in mourning. He mourned the loss, at his own hands, of his beloved mother and only caring companion. Three days into mourning, he shaved his head with a razor blade and applied palm oil on it. He wept bitterly every day of that week, begging for his mother's mercy and forgiveness. It fully dawned on him that he had committed an egregious and unwarranted crime, and that nothing he did would reverse his utter foolishness. While he mourned, he turned down

Dibong's repeated requests for hunting expeditions.

On the eighth day, Bim went to the river and thoroughly bathed himself and put on a new outfit. He then went over to Dibong's, who instantly noticed the change in his friend's countenance.

"Bim, I haven't seen you in days! But you look so sad and miserable! Your face is drawn, your cheeks are sunken, and you look hungry and sulky. Tell me, what's the matter? We *are* pals, and we should be there for each other, shouldn't we? How can I help you?" Bim sighed in resignation, and then said,

"Thank you, Dibong, but never mind. You cannot help with this problem." Dibong was ostensibly taken aback, but feigned ignorance of why his friend might be so out of sorts. Both walked off silently to the forest, each with a catapult strapped to the neck and a raffia-palm bag strapped to the left shoulder. As before, they were out hunting for birds and rodents, now increasingly their staple meal. Dibong was a better hunter and, within an hour, had caught a squirrel and a hare; Bim had succeeded in downing only a sunbird. They were both perspiring intensely.

Noon was fast approaching, so Dibong once more excused himself with the usual promise of coming back shortly afterwards. Bim trailed him surreptitiously as he headed for the shade tree. This time, Bim meant to register the lyrics and tone of the signature song carefully. Again, and in pain, he listened as Dibong sang:

Mother, Mother, give me food to eat.
And then of Bim I will go ask:
"Where have you left your mother?"

The following day, Bim and Dibong met in the forest by mid-morning. They had agreed to hunt for a while and then set traps for the bigger animals. When it was time to set the traps, Bim told his friend that he had forgotten his gun at home and asked Dibong to keep working while he rushed back home for it. Upon saying this, he scrammed. Having mastered the lyrics of his friend's plea for food from his mother, he went straight to the shade tree and sang:

Mother, Mother, give me food to eat.
And then of Bim I will go ask:
"Where have you left your mother?"

Convinced it was her son's voice, she took out food to drop for him, and Bim instantly caught her by the hand and dragged her down. They struggled a little before Bim finally hacked her to death. Bim returned to the forest, where he rejoined his companion for what looked like just another day of hunting till sunset, when they parted ways. Dibong returned home and found his mother dead, but did not take long to figure out that he had just been paid in his coin.

10

REVENGE OF THE COASTER
(OR HOW A WITCH TOOK ADVANTAGE
OF A HELPLESS WOMAN)
[Narrated by Jerry Rawlings Nshuhnkum]

THERE once lived a man and his wife. They had been married not very long, and the man, called Akongnwi, began to wonder how he would provide for his family should they be blessed with a child. He decided to travel to the coastal region of the country, where colonialism had begun to take root. There were many job opportunities, and Akongnwi was determined to make money. Before leaving, he told his wife, Ikam, "As I am leaving, I fear that our baby will arrive before I return. Before you go into labor, stand up and face south—in the direction of the coast—and call out for me."

The pains of labor came rather abruptly, and Ikam forgot the instructions she had been given. Instead of facing south, she faced north and called out for her husband. Forth came a fierce-looking woman whose teeth stuck out like the fingers of a giant. She was called Dzediwen, and she carried a large basket of pumpkins on her head and ordered the expecting woman to get off the chair and help her lower the load to the ground. In pain and with much difficulty, Ikam came to Dzediwen's help.

Over the next days, Dzediwen gave orders to her hostess without regard for her physical condition. The intruder hurled insults at Ikam, whom she had fetching water and firewood and cooking for her everyday. Even after Ikam's baby-boy arrived, none of that treatment changed. Each time Dzediwen returned from the farm, she asked Ikam to drop her piece of log of a baby and help her lower the load she brought back from the farm.

Ikam would comply helplessly, laying her baby on the bed and helping the woman.

Akongnwi had long been waiting for a call from his wife and wondered why she had not called. A year had passed since he left, so he decided to come back home to find out for himself what might have gone wrong. He returned home to find his wife beleaguered and emaciated from the torments she had endured. The culprit was at the farm. Furious, he vowed to pay Dzediwen back in kind. He went to a next-door neighbor's, Taambo, and borrowed an axe. Towards sunset he took his position behind the door in wait for the uninvited guest, for that is what *Dzediwen* means.

When Dzediwen arrived she ordered Ikam as she had previously, although this time with a threat: "Drop your piece of log and come help me lower this load or I'll break your bones!"

"I have had it with you and will not put down my son. He is *not* a piece of log!"

Dzediwen, taken aback and almost convinced Ikam was drunk, dropped the load and charged at her host like a bull. Ikam retreated indoors, and, as Dzediwen was about to pounce on her, an axe came down on the prowler's back, and she fell back screaming helplessly. She then got up dazed and took flight, with the axe still stuck to her back.

When Taambo learned about the incident, his main worry was his axe, which he feared might be gone for good. He warned Akongnwi: "That axe is my most priced possession, and I cannot live without it. You better go and bring it back." He rejected monetary compensation and all locally made replacement axes that he was offered, leaving Akongnwi with no choice but to recover the axe.

After a morning's trek, he arrived at a farm which had a lot of fresh produce, including large, luscious garden eggs. The garden eggs were irresistible and made him salivate, but he didn't want to steal them. As he contemplated his options, a child suddenly showed up. Akongnwi confessed to him his craving for the garden eggs and asked where the farmer was so he might beg for some. The boy led him to an old sorceress, who allowed him to pick some of the fruits. He got enough for a few days. He also disclosed to the woman his primary quest—recovery of an axe from Dzediwen. The farmer gave him some more garden eggs, a pot of slime, and road directions. He put away some of the garden eggs and wrapped the rest.

When Akongnwi arrived at Dzediwen's he found the aching witch in her kitchen and presented her with garden eggs and tadpoles as an expression of his sympathy for her *accident*. She relished them so much that she relaxed and began to share with her guest personal stories, including how she sustained an injury on her back.

"How was the axe removed?" Akongnwi inquired.

"A skilled medicine-man took it out. That may have saved my life," she smirked with relief.

"Where's the axe," Akongnwi pressed on.

Dzediwen pointed to the barn, whence an axe stuck out. He recognized it as the very weapon he had planted in the woman's back and began to think of a strategy for making away with it. As soon as Dzediwen stepped away and into an inner room, Akongnwi leapt to his feet, grabbed the axe, and was off to the races. Dzediwen, unable to pursue him, uttered a shrill cry to his children, who were in the backyard.

The fast-footed boys gave chase as Akongnwi headed

towards the sorceress's home. They were fast closing in on him when he took out the slime and spread it on the narrow road. Once the pursuers stepped on the slime, they each took a heavy fall and gave up the pursuit. Akongnwi went on to the sorceress's and thanked her for her assistance. She in turn congratulated him on a job well done and asked him to pick some more garden eggs for his family on his way back. He picked five.

The following morning Taambo came to ask for his axe when Akongnwi had left for the farm. After looking around for a while, he helped himself to a garden egg and left. When Akongnwi returned, he noticed that one of his garden eggs was missing. His wife reported that it was eaten by Taambo. Vexed about his neighbor's audaciousness, he vowed to make him pay for it.

A few moments later, Taambo returned. Akongnwi pointed to the axe and asked him whether he had seen it. He concurred, adding that he meant to regain possession of it formally. He also confirmed having eaten his garden egg.

"My garden egg!" screamed Akongnwi. "How dare you? I want the *same* garden egg, and right away!"

Taambo went in search of a garden egg when he came to an expansive farm full of succulent garden eggs. It was the sorceress's farm. He said to himself, "Isn't this the farm whence Akongnwi picked the garden eggs? Why did he pick only five? I'll get myself a bagful of them!" He began filling his *mokota* bag with garden eggs when a child came by and asked him whether he had secured permission for the harvest. He responded snappishly,

"Don't you bother me! Are there no elders in your family?"

Taking heart, the boy responded, "This farm belongs

to my mother. If you need garden eggs, please come with me and ask my mother." Taambo became more temperate and followed the child. As they entered the woman's house, she asked the trespasser, "Is it true that you have been to my farm and harvested my garden eggs?" He agreed, and she inquired further, "By the way, what was your destination?"

"I was headed to Dzediwen's," he answered. She gave him directions. When he arrived, Dzediwen immediately pounced on him, saying,

"Are you here to complete your brother's mission? He came here and stole my axe, and you are back for another trick, right?" Before he could break free, Dzediwen decapitated him.

11

THE FARMER AND THE CANNIBAL
[Narrated by Mami Anna Anwanwen Ayuninjam]

ONCE upon a time a woman went farming with her four children. It was a beautiful day, and they looked forward to a long day of work. No sooner had they settled down to work than the weather changed and the sky became overcast with a huge dark cloud, and then it began to rain. The family of five sought shelter under a big tree, hoping the rain would soon stop and they would resume work, but the skies would not let off. The rain poured with ever increasing intensity, and the woman decided she and her children should seek a more secure shelter. The woman raised her head and saw a hut close to the farm. She took her children there for shelter, hoping to resume work after the torrential downpour.

As they entered the hut, they found a man sitting inside. He had overgrown hair which came way down his body, covering his face and abdomen. He looked dejected. The hut was cold and gloomy and seemed uninhabited, safe for this grumpy and lonesome man. However, as he saw the strangers come in he was in high spirits. He seemed not to have eaten in days; yet he was so happy to see the family he could hardly conceal his joy. His smile unveiled two pairs of giant claws sticking out from his bright red upper and lower gums. That was all he had for teeth. The woman then realized she had just made a big mistake; she had just brought her family to a cannibal.

How would she extricate herself and the children for the cannibal's fangs, she wondered. The children were utterly oblivious of their mother's predicament and seemed simply happy to be sheltered. To keep warm, the woman gathered wood from the porch and made a fire. The children closed in around the hearth and enjoyed the heart-warming flames.

The children began to sense the mysterious air of the

old man's hut, but they stuck together, close to their mother. Then she turned and looked at the man with *pity* and told one of her children,

"Your father's hair is unkempt and looks pitiful. Why don't you go and fetch a pair of scissors so I can give him a clean look?" As the child left, she nudged and signaled him not to come back. This child heeded the advice and went for good. She waited for a while and, *impatient*, sighed as she wondered out loud why the child was taking so long. She then sent a second child, her only daughter, to go and find out what was holding the first. As this one left, she again beckoned her not to return. She too heeded her mother's advice and went for good.

After a while, she called the third child, Aze, and sent him after his siblings. Aze was the black sheep of the family. He turned and looked at his mother with spite, coiled back, and said he felt too cold to step outside.

"Why is it always I?" he whined. "Chi is right next to me; why don't you send him?"

Totally unsurprised at Aze's behavior, the woman sent her fourth child for a pair of scissors. And as he left, he responded to his mother's signal to not come back to the hut.

Aze, his mother, and the fearsome host then remained in the hut. There was grave silence for a while. The mother broke the silence with another sigh as she softened her voice and begged Aze to go and check on his siblings. Her plea fell on deaf ears as he again refused, groaned, and went into the old man's bedroom, saying it was still raining, he was cold, and he would rather lie down. He found comfort under the old man's bed. Unable to persuade Aze, the mother sighed again, saying to the man she was going to find out what was wrong with the *stubborn* children she had sent. The man waited in vain for the return of the departed mother and the three children and went to bed, forgetting about the fourth child. While he slept, the child pocked him repeatedly with a sharp stick. He got up and wondered to himself,

"I have watched game come into my house leave. What type of bug might be stinging me this much?" He made a fire and, with a fire-brand, looked under the bed and found the child hiding there. He grabbed and roasted him like a rat-mole and devoured him that same night.

12

THE SEARCH FOR MR. HANDSOME
[Narrated by Joseph Che'for Ashing]

THERE once lived a girl called Nge, an only child and the pride of her parents, who were wealthy traders. They took great care of their daughter and acceded to her every wish. Nge was dazzlingly pretty, and, as she grew older, boys' eyes followed her wherever she went. Having no siblings and thinking that everyone else was beneath her station, Nge did not understand or appreciate the important, less tangible aspects of life such as friendship, kindness, and respect.

Nge's sixteenth birthday was celebrated with pomp. The entire village was treated to exquisite cuisine and day-long entertainment. The ceremony also marked her coming of age, and she had to get married and start a family as the only way of bringing pride to her parents. Nge was known to virtually all her fellow villagers, and the lavish celebration only gained her more acquaintances.

For months following Nge's sixteenth birthday celebration, boys and parents swamped her compound-- the boys seeking her hand in marriage, and the parents seeking a wife for their son. Yet a smaller number of elderly men were there in their own behalf, seeking a second, third, or fourth wife. Thus, there was fierce competition among the village youths for Nge's love. But as often as men proposed to this beauty, she found something on which to fault her suitors. They were too short or too tall, too skinny or too plump faced, too smart and scary or too sheepish and idiotic to be her children's father. Most suitors, however, were dismissed on very simple grounds: they did not look handsome, were of poor parentage did not look properly dressed, or did not wear jewelry. For these and similar reasons, Nge turned down hundreds of men who would otherwise be husbands.

Eventually men stopped coming to ask for Nge's hand in marriage; her cold receptions became common knowledge across the village. People now seemed interested in knowing who would eventually marry her, since she had rejected all of the village's young men.

Then an unknown bachelor learned of the would-be bride who would yield only to a man smooth as gold and bright as the sun. This bachelor, by the name of Nang, lived at the bottom of a lake, in the northernmost part of the village. He did not eat fish or tadpoles; he lived on human flesh and blood, as did everyone else in this marine habitat. He and all other under-water inhabitants were headless and armless, and whenever they needed these body parts, they had to borrow them for short periods of time.

Nang set off on his trip to propose to Nge on a market-day. He had no head, no legs, and no clothes, but he had a good plan, a very good plan. When he emerged from the water, he saw a man standing by the lake. Nang borrowed his head and arms and promised to return them a little later at the same spot. The bystander agreed and lent his head and arms to Nang.

Now, Nang needed clothes. It was noon, and many shoppers were still streaming to the weekly market and looked well dressed. He stopped one of them and borrowed his shoes, a pair of pants, and a beautiful shirt. As before, he promised to return them a little later, and the lender agreed to sit by and wait until Nang came back. The next pedestrian he saw was dressed in a suit and dripped with jewelry. Nang borrowed from him a jacket, a pretty tie, a cowry necklace, and some gold rings. He could not walk into Nge's compound; he needed a car! He flagged down a little sporty car that had no passengers; it would leave a lasting impression on Nge, he was convinced. In the car were sun glasses and a black hat, both of which he gladly put on. Nang was set to visit the prodigy of beauty. He looked young, sharp, and spiffy, and certainly very tempting, even to Nge.

Nge's compound was large and fenced all around. It was separated from the highway by a long pavement. Her family knew someone was coming minutes before the suitor reached the main gate, because the family dog suddenly began to bark furiously and run around the compound as if it was mad. Nge and her parents were home when the suitor arrived, but he could barely get through the gate as the dog would not stop trying to rip off his clothes. The dog's behavior took everyone by surprise, for it had been very cordial towards all the other unsuccessful suitors. Nge's parents tried desperately to restrain it and apologized repeatedly to their guest for the dog's embarrassing manners.

Out of frustration, Nge tethered the dog to a pole in the backyard. Nang told Nge's parents he came to offer his hand in marriage to their beautiful daughter. They responded as they had on numerous other occasions:

"We have no particular objections. The final word is Nge's."

The stir created by the dog so alarmed Nge's aunts and uncles that they strongly urged her to turn down Nang's offer. She insisted that she had seen her man and would follow him to the ends of the earth; nothing, not even the dog, would stop her from marrying her man. She added,

"He looks handsome and classy and is the right man for me. If I didn't marry him, I will die a spinster."

Even Nge's parents soon joined the other dissenting voices, but they too could not get their daughter to reconsider her choice, although they would rather she married the devil's son than remain unmarried. Finally, and in frustration, Nge's father told her that she was making a personal choice and must be willing to live with the consequences.

"If your marriage turns out badly, you will have yourself alone to blame; we completely oppose your marrying this young man. If, however, your marriage turns out good (and we'll have you in our prayers) and you bear children, you are welcome back home anytime you choose to visit and show us your children."

As a wedding present Nge's parents gave her the family dog. It took several persons to get the dog into the car, for it would not go willingly; it barked and scraped at anyone trying to make it part of the marriage, but finally it was forced in, and the newly wedded couple took off.

After a few moments' drive, Nang pulled off the street as he came to the car owner, who had been waiting impatiently. Nang apologized for the delay, returned his car keys, hat, and sun glasses, and then tipped him. Nge was perplexed and felt a cold chill run down her spine. They had to walk the rest of the way. A little further ahead, Nang saw the man who had lent him a jacket, a tie, a necklace, and gold rings and returned his belongings, yet with an apology and one clove of a cola nut for a tip. Next he returned the shoes, pants, and shirt. Nang was now stark naked and held the weeping beauty queen firmly as she tried to break loose. Finally, when they got to the lakeside, Nang returned the head and arms to the waiting lender, and again with an apology and a tip of one full cola nut. Nge, unable to run away *from* her captor groom, entered the lake with him. The dog broke free and barked as it ran all the way home.

13

THE TORTOISE AND THE CHIEF (OR HOW THE TORTOISE GAINED RESPECT AS THE MOST INTELLIGENT OF ANIMALS)
[Narrated by Mami Julie Tantoh]

A TORTOISE had a baby and decided to withhold naming the child till he was of age. When time came, she named him Sense Pass King, which means "wiser than the king."

The village chief heard about this young tortoise and asked him to come and shave his head. The tortoise left with roasted corn on the cob, which he kept in his bag. The hair job seemed to be interminable as the tortoise took his time and worked pretentiously. An hour had gone by with no end in sight, so the chief asked impatiently,

"Why is the hair job taking this long?"

"I am right on target," said the tortoise. "Here is some fresh corn for you. It should help lessen the tedium. I want to ensure you have a superb haircut." The man enjoyed the corn and became less peevish.

When the young tortoise finished, the chief asked him to gather and throw away the hair he had trimmed from his head. The young tortoise did. Then in a sudden turn, the chief said to the tortoise, "Sense Pass King, why have you discarded my hair? I want it back on my head!"

"Return my corn, and I will replace your hair," responded Sense Pass King.

The chief pleaded, "My friend, we cannot get into a squabble. When you leave the palace tonight, I will give you some cargo to keep for me." He then went outside and returned with a goat, which Sense Pass King took home.

A few months later, the goat bore lambs, and the chief asked Sense Pass King to take the lambs to the market. Sense Pass King retorted,

"You gave me a goat, not a sheep. Don't lambs come from sheep?"

The chief insisted that goats did bear offspring, but, unable to convince Sense Pass King otherwise, he took Sense Pass King to court. Prior to the hearing, Sense Pass King went to his father and complained about the case. His father calmed him and assured him of his full support.

On the day of the hearing, Sense Pass King and his father left for the courthouse late in the afternoon. The courthouse was both an administrative headquarters and a social gathering place. As they approached the courthouse, fellow-villagers assaulted Sense Pass King's father for his discourtesy:

"For a case involving the chief, why did you choose to appear this late? Are you hear to postpone the hearing or to attend it?"

"Please calm down and don't be upset with me," he answered. "I have a revelation for you all."

The chief was so upset he could barely contain himself, but was persuaded to give the man a chance. Sense Pass King's father addressed the throng:

"My brothers and sisters, on my way here, I witnessed something really puzzling. I saw a male deer having babies, so I stopped to help him. He had twins. If I ignored him and he died in labor or had a still birth, how could I ever live with myself? Wouldn't I have hurt God and our ancestors as well? After delivering the twins, I took them and the father deer home and cleaned and fed them before coming here, unsure of meeting anyone. I am glad you are still here."

The chief rose in outrage and told Sense Pass King's father, "Stop that nonsense! What are you talking about? Do males give birth?" Sense Pass King's father rose in anger and retorted,

"Listen, listen, listen!" Facing the jury, he continued, "Why does the chief have the audacity to ask such a question? Is he the only one who may ask my son to bring him lambs born of a goat, but no one may claim to have seen a male deer bearing children?"

Then a lion got up and asked Sense Pass King himself, "You who walk shakily, will you now claim victory after keeping the whole village waiting for you all day? I propose we settle the matter by a tug of war."

Sense Pass King agreed, asking that they go near a river, where he might take cover as he could stand the blazing heat of the sun. He added, "You may stay off shore since you are much bigger than I." The lion agreed, took one end of the rope to the riverside, and attached it to the root of a tree. The lion had the other end, which he wrapped around his neck. Sense Pass King, invisible to anyone, asked the lion to pull. The lion pulled. Sense Pass King could feel the rope becoming more taut as the lion struggled to hold his ground. Suddenly, the rope became floppy and dropped to the ground. Sense Pass King got out and found that the lion had choked to death.

A deer arrived on the scene and mocked the dead lion, saying, "How could a mere tortoise kill a lion, king of the forest? That couldn't happen to me!" Then he challenged Sense Pass King, asking him, "Can you even race me?" Sense Pass King responded,

"I am fair game," stretching and retracting his neck in confidence. To make the challenge irresistible, he added, "If you and I were to race to that hill on the horizon, I would be there and back while you were still on your first leg."

The whole village assembled to watch a race between the tortoise and the deer. On the day of the race, the tortoise placed his friends on the entire race course. At the sound of the whistle, the contestants took off. Before long, the deer was way ahead and called out for the tortoise, which responded,

"I'm right ahead."

A few hundred yards later, the deer called out again to brag about his separation from the tortoise, but heard the same response from ahead, spurring the deer to gallop even faster, trying to *catch up* with his challenger. The race took the contestants across the entire breadth of the village, and they were already deep inside the next village. Every few hundred yards, the deer called out the tortoise to blow his own horn, but each time he was deflated when the tortoise mockingly said he was *ahead* of the deer.

As the runners neared the next outer frontier, the deer was still *behind*, exhausted, and dehydrated, and when the deer arrived at the boundary, it could barely walk. Soon it collapsed and died.

The nearby tortoise came back, removed a horn from the deer's head, and made a flute from it with which he chanted:

Here's my horn;
It's blowing.
Here's my horn;
It's blowing for real.

Here's my horn;
It's singing.

Here's my horn;
It's singing for real.

Here's my horn;
It's talking.
Here's my horn;
It's talking for real.

All the other animals came out, and then acknowledged the tortoise as the most intelligent of beings in the animal kingdom. No other animal would dare to disparage the tortoise ever again.

14

THE UNCOOPERATIVE SONS
[Narrated by Jerry Rawlings Nshuhnkum]

A LONG time ago, a man lived with his two sons. They were both of marriage age, but continued to live with their parents because of frequent family disagreements regarding succession, with each son claiming the right. These disputes led to frequent fist fights.

The man had reached a ripe old age and was quickly losing his physical energies and felt that death was imminent. He, however, feared that after he passed on, the rivalry might intensify and further destabilize the family.

One day he became ill and asked his sons to go and fetch him firewood. They were each to tie their wood in a bundle of five pieces. When they returned, the man asked his first son to place his bundle of wood on his laps and break it in half. He tried in vain. The man turned to the other son and gave him the same instructions. He too failed.

The man then asked both sons to pool forces and break the wood together, one bundle at a time. In the same order, the older son paced his bundle of wood on his laps, and, with all four hands coming down simultaneously, the boys split the bundle in two. The younger son placed his own bundle of wood, which he and his brother again split with ease. The ailing man turned to his sons and, taking a deep breath, asked,

"Do you know why the wood broke?" without letting

them answer, he went on with difficulty, "Because of your cooperation, your joint efforts. Why are you brothers? What examples will you set for your own children? You pooled your energies and accomplished a task neither of you could alone. If you continue to work together, you will find success; if you choose to fight each other and go it alone, you will encounter insurmountable obstacles. You know which route to take. I have nothing more to tell you."

The man got up and, with the help of an old cane, walked unsteadily to bedroom for his afternoon nap. When the sons returned at sundown to check on their father, he was dead. The boys resolved to set aside their differences and work together. Their businesses soon began to yield abundantly as their clientele grew in leaps and bounds.

15

THE FARMER AND THE GOAT HERDER

[Narrated by Mami Julie Tantoh]

THERE once lived a farmer whose cornfield was frequented by goats. His farm was fenced, but somehow goats always made their way into it and ate the corn. For long he wondered how the goats got in.

One night he went to the farm and mounted guard. At mid-night he saw a man slide down a rope from the sky and land on the farm. He had a goat with him. He was soon followed by several other men, each with a goat, which they loosed on the farm to graze. The farmer watched with consternation.

Once the goats had had their fill, the farmer grabbed one of them and slaughtered it. As the party left, one of the men could not find his goat and so walked around the farm searching for it. At the edge of the farm he saw the farmer sitting next to the decapitated goat and told him with regret,

"Oh my goat!" To this the farmer responded,

"Oh my testicles!" Upon uttering these words, the head of the goat was instantly affixed onto the farmer's face, while the goat herder's testicles dropped. That night the herder and his friends search for anyone who could cure the testicular disease, but came up empty. He returned to the farmer and offered to remove the goat's head from the farmer's face if the farmer would treat his testicular disease. They agreed and each kept his word and dispelled the other's hex.

The goat herder went a short distance from the farm and wondered to himself just *where* he was going without his goat and murmured,

"Oh my goat!" to which the farmer replied,

"Oh my testicles!" As before, the goat's head was reattached to the farmer's face, while the goat herder's testicles dropped and dangled between his legs. The goat herder returned to the farmer and again asked for a cure in exchange for ridding him of the goat's head. Once more, both men freed each other of the anathemas.

As the goat herder neared his home, he wondered how he could live without his goat and said under his breath,

"Oh my goat!" to which the farmer responded,

"Oh my testicles!" That said, the farmer once more found himself bearing the head of a goat, while the herder's testicles dropped. Day was fast dawning, and the goat herder could not afford to be seen in his condition; yet he could not return to the farmer to ask for help. Letting his companions go home without him, he transformed himself into a dry log of wood and lay on the roadside.

The next day his friends came by and found him, but treated the site as a curiosity. When other passers-by noticed the log of wood, they set it on fire, and the other herders exclaimed,

"The man's head is on fire!" and ran away. With his death the goat's head also left the farmer's face, goats no longer grazed in his farm, and he finally harvested his corn.

16

THE COCOYAM FARMER WHO ACCEPTED PAYMENT IN FLESH
[Narrated by Mami Julie Tantoh]

A COCOYAM farmer once met a tadpole fisherman and asked him what he ate while fishing. He said his only concern was the tadpoles and that he ate nothing. The farmer offered him a yam which he had in his bag. The man gladly accepted and ate the yam hungrily. The farmer then told him,

> *Pay, oh pay my yam!*
> *A yam given me by a harp maker*
> *A harp maker who broke my walking stick*
> *A walking stick I inherited from my father*
> *My father, a descendant of Beche*
> *Beche, the offspring of Njeleh*
> *Whose bag dropped pam!*
> *And was scooped up chwet!*

The fisherman gave him a tadpole, and he continued on his way and met mourners who were still grieving over the loss of a loved one. He asked them what they ate while mourning, and they said they had had nothing, so he offered them the tadpole. As soon as they finished eating it, the farmer said,

> *Pay, oh pay my tadpole!*
> *A tadpole given me by a fisherman*
> *A fisherman who ate my yam*
> *A yam given me by a harp maker*
> *A harp maker who broke my walking stick*

A walking stick I inherited from my father
My father, a descendant of Beche
Beche, the offspring of Njeleh
Whose bag dropped pam!
And was scooped up chwet!

The mourners were taken aback and told the farmer they could not pay him, but led him to the grave of the deceased to prove that they were indeed bereaved. The farmer would not accept any excuses, and so dug up the corpse and carried it away. When he arrived at a river, he said,

Oh river so pure and calm!
Flow up and flow down
So I can pass
With this beautiful baby of ours.

The water stopped flowing momentarily and separated—one half flowing upwards and another continuing downwards, enabling the man to cross. He got to another river and made the same plea:

Oh river so pure and calm!
Flow up and flow down
So I can pass
With this beautiful baby of ours.

Like the first one, this river also separated, and the man crossed it. He got to a stream and said to himself,

"Am I going to keep pleading with every little body of water just for safe passage?" As soon as he stepped into the stream, he was swept away by an undercurrent he had not suspected. He and the corpse were stopped downstream by a hunter's trap. When the hunter arrived and tried to catch what he thought was game, the farmer

91

said,

Come nearer, come nearer!
Child circumciser, adult circumciser!

The hunter ran back home and told his neighbor about an animal he tried to remove from his trap that spoke to him. The neighbor returned to the stream with him, and the entrapped farmer repeated his threat:

Come nearer, come nearer!
Child circumciser, adult circumciser!

Both men ran off, wondering what type of animal could be speaking like humans. The men came back holding a bundle of spears. The farmer threatened to sever boys' and men's genitals, but the hunter advanced gently. The farmer raised his hand and exposed a red armpit. The hunter threw the spear, and it entered the armpit. The farmer raised the other hand, and the hunter shot another spear which penetrated the armpit, and the entrapped man slumped backwards into the water and died. The two corpses were extricated from the trap and taken to the chief's palace for identification and internment.